I0548169

Manifested

Dreams

Copyright © [2019] by [Dr. Yvonne Johnson]
All rights reserved. No part of this book may be reproduced, scanned,
or distributed in any printed or electronic form without permission.
First Edition: [June 2020]
Printed in the United States of America
ISBN: [978-1-7352593-0-7]

Table of Contents

I am my ancestors' wildest dream

Shaili Ja Ma. 2017

Lost Treasure.

May 16, 2015 was a dreary and rainy day and I listened to the pity-patter of raindrops on the roof and windows. My mother called me to help with packing up my grandmother's belongings; she died two weeks ago. I have always dreaded this day.

I closed my eyes and could still see her smiling face. Her skin was smooth and dark brown. It reminds me of the color of the bark of the Magnolia trees that grew in her backyard. Her hair was long and gray. She kept it in a long, single braid that hung down her back. On special occasions, she would wrap her braid around her head and wear it like a crown. She looked like a queen. She was a small woman, but do not let her size fool you. She was quite strong. Her eyes sparkled like the stars in the sky on a clear night. Even when she started to get sick and weak, her eyes still shined till the day she closed them for the last time.

My grandmother always shared stories about our family history. Now that she had passed, I wish I had paid more attention to the stories she had shared with me. She was always so animated during her storytelling sessions. Her stories were filled with details of how life was for her parents and their many ancestors before them. I used to wonder how she could remember all those stories. She always said we came from a long line of storytellers. She would say,

"Khari was your great, great, great, great grandfather who was the village griot in Africa."

1

The griot was the African storyteller for their village. A griot would keep oral history and pass them down from one generation to the next. She told me that the people in the village would rely on him track the history of the village. He was well respected. She always told me,

"You should be proud to be a Johnson. You come from a long line of strong, intelligent people."

She would stick her chest out as she said it. You could hear the pride in her voice. I always could feel that same pride fills me up every single time she said this to me.

My mother walked into my bedroom and said,

"It is time to go, Amari. I know you don't want to go, baby, but Mommy needs you right now."

I moaned, "Yeah, I know."

I slowly walked out of my room. I needed to be strong for my mother, but I secretly hoped I could deal with being back in my grandmother's house. She would not be there to greet me. My mother and I got into the car. Since my grandmother died, my mother always looked so tired. She used to have the same bright eyes as my grandmother, but they were now sad and gloomy. I could often hear her crying in her room at night. My Dad would try to comfort her, but it never worked. I knew that she missed her mother because I missed her too.

While my mother was driving, I tried to think of a way to lift her spirits.

"Hey, mom," I said.

"Yes, Amari," she replied."

"I got an 'A' on my last math test."

"Wow, Amari, which is great. I'm so proud of you."

I was hoping I could put a smile on her face. She briefly smiled, but you could still tell her mind was somewhere else. As we pulled up to my grandmother's house, I started to feel nervous for some reason. My Aunt Janet and Uncle Jamal were already there packing. I spoke to everyone and waited on the couch for instructions on what they wanted me to do. My mother asked me to help my cousin Elsie fold some clothes.

Elsie had long hair and skin like my grandmother. Sometimes, she wore her hair in a single long braid like her. Today she had her hair in two braids. Elsie and I shared our fondest memories of our grandmother. Elsie said,

"I still don't believe that she is gone."

I sighed, "Yeah me either. I did not want to come here today. I keep waiting for her to come into the room and tell us we are not folding the clothes right."

"Yeah, she would say 'See, baby first, you must do this and then do that. Now that is the proper way to fold a shirt'." Both of us smiled because we both knew that if she were here, that would be just what she would do. In my mind, I could still hear her voice.

I heard my Uncle Jamal yelling,

"Hey y'all! What is this?" We all came running to the den.

"I found this box, and it has a lot of old letters in it. Yeah, some of these letters look really old."

Uncle Jamal tried to blow the dust off one of the letters as He silently read it to himself. "Hey, it seems like these are some of the stories momma used to tell us. I always wondered how she could remember all that information. She was like a walking history book."

Uncle Jamal asked us what we should do with the letters.

"I know that they are unbelievably valuable. I do not want to throw them away." I asked my mother if I could keep them. I felt that it would be like having a piece of my grandmother with me. I already missed hearing her tell me stories about our family. Everyone agreed that I should keep the box. My mother said that the letters were precious to the family and that I should ensure that I kept them in a safe place.

After hours of packing up my grandmother's items, my mother and I drove back home. My father and sister saw the box I brought to the house and asked,

"What's in the box, Amari?"

"Our family history," I answered.

4

"Family history?" my father asked with a puzzled look on his face.

"Yeah, in the box. I have letters from different family members."

With a puzzled expression, my sister Imani asked, "Who are the letters from? Are there letters from Grandma and Grandpa?"

"I am not sure yet but, once I start reading some of the letters, I will let you know" I replied. I placed the box inside the closest in my bedroom. I was too tired to start reading that night, but I could not wait for the morning to come so I could start reading the letters.

The next morning, I got up and ate breakfast. After I finished, I asked my mother if I could go to my room and start reading the Grandma's letters.

***

The first letter I read was about a girl named Sallie. She was born a slave on Davies Plantation in Tennessee. Sallie's first entry in her letter stated that she did not learn how to read and write until she was much older, she wanted to start writing about her experiences as a little girl with hopes that her children will keep her family's story alive.

Sallie:

My first memory was when I lost my best friend, Mary. She and her mother were carried off to the auction block to be sold. Mary and I were playing together just yesterday. We often talked about and imagined what life would be if we were free. We would live in a big house like Master John. We would wear fancy clothes like Miss Jane, his wife. I often wondered if we would ever be free. Could Colored Folks own a house like Master John? Ma told me there were free Colored Folks up North. I wonder what kind of houses they lived in. She always said trouble does not last forever. That one day we will be free. I really hope we will be able to see that day.

Later that day, I saw a strange man talking to Master John. I later found out that he was a slave owner. I did not know he was going to take my best friend, Mary. That day I wondered why Mary and the other slaves were on the other side of the field, and the strange man was walking around them as if he was inspecting them. The strange man took Mary and put her and his other new slaves on the back of his wagon, I could not stop crying. Ma tried to make me be quiet, but I just could not stop crying. Master John yelled at my Ma, telling her to stop me from crying. I cried so hard I could no longer make a sound. I knew it would be the last time I would see my friend. I could not understand why they had to go. That day was different for me. I walked around in a daze. I went about my daily chores of picking up the trash and carrying water to the people in the field.

After a long day, I went home. Ma overheard Master John talking to his guest. He told the guest that President Lincoln signed the Emancipation Proclamation that should go into effect on January 1st the next year, 1863. The Emancipation Proclamation will free all slaves within the rebellious states. Master John's guest laughed and said,

"You know Andrew Johnson will not go for that."

Andrew Johnson was the governor of Tennessee.

"Hopefully, we can be free." Ma said. After that, I had a little glimpse of hope. I heard some other slaves saying that the country was fighting. The North was at war with the South. They called it the Civil War.

On the 24th of October 1864, Governor Johnson freed the slaves in Tennessee. Andrew Johnson was originally against freeing the slaves but eventually freed slaves in Tennessee. Sam, one of the field slaves, came by while we were sleeping to tell us that Johnson freed the slaves. He kept saying,

"We are free. We are free!!"

Pa looked at him in disbelief. We overheard cheers and shouting from the other slave quarters. I still could not believe it. I thought I was dreaming. We were all confused. We were still waiting Master John to give us permission to leave, we did not know if we should go North, or how we would go.

8

The next morning, Ma and Pa were trying to figure out what freedom would look like for us. The newfound freedom brought about joy, excitement, fear, and disappointment. Many of the slaves were planning to travel to the North to make a better life for themselves. I thought about Mary. I wondered if she was free. I wondered if she were just as excited as I was and if we could finally be free like we were in our dreams. Pa and Ma knew that traveling to the North would not be that easy. Many plantation owners did not want to accept that Governor Johnson had freed the slaves, and in some areas in the South, the slaves were not free, and the Civil War was still going on.

A few months after the slaves in Tennessee were freed, news spread that Abraham Lincoln was assassinated. That was on April 15, 1865. Many freed slaves questioned how this would affect their freedom. Andrew Johnson was later sworn in as the next President. President Andrew Johnson kept his true feeling towards Slavery and did not enforce southern states to grant freedom to former slaves. The Republicans tried to push reconstruction policies.

Ma and Pa decided not to travel north. Pa decided to go out and find work. Pa was skilled at working the fields and building wagons. After Slavery, several states created Black Codes. Black Codes gave newly freed slaves the right to marry, own land, and sue in court, but they were not able to testify against whites nor serve on a jury. Some newly freed slaves became sharecroppers and they continued to work on former slave owners' land but were paid part of the crop for rent. Pa did not want to do that, but it was difficult for him to find work.

Many White Folks did not want to pay newly freed slaves for their labor. Ma was an excellent cook. Master John agreed to allow us to stay in our quarters in exchange for her to continue working for him and Miss Jane. Pa did not like the idea of Ma working for the Davies. After several unsuccessful attempts of Pa trying to find a job, he traveled to Fort Pickering to enlist in the Army. Ma did not want Pa to join the Army but said he wanted to fight with the hope of making life better for us. Pa said he had heard how many newly freed slaves transitioned from Slavery to freedom by joining the Army and that he thought it would be a good idea. Pa joined and Ma was also able to join the Army as a cook. Many Colored soldiers got education through joining the Army. Pa was excited when he started learning how to read. He would come home and try to teach us what he had learned. Pa seemed immensely proud of himself. Even though Pa was teaching me what he learned, I still wanted to go to school. Pa promised me that I will be able to go to school one day, soon.

On April 30, 1866, many Colored Soldiers were removed from the Army. Pa said that the Unit Leader told his unit that since the war was over, their services were not needed anymore. Upon their dismissal, the Colored Soldiers wanted their discharge pay. It was rumored that the soldiers were planning to seek retaliation against the white soldiers. I overheard Pa talking to some neighbors about the plans of retaliation; I had to hide so Pa would not see me. I prayed that no one would get hurt. Tensions were rising in Memphis. Many Whites felt that Colored Folks should not been given the opportunity to join the Army because it would give them the confidence to demand more rights.

On May 1, 1866, the police approached some Colored soldiers who were gathered. The police tried to arrest the Colored Soldiers, but several Colored Folks saw what was going on and protested their arrest. Gunshots rang out and left several Colored

People injured, some dead. Mayor Park refused to request assistance in controlling the violence in Memphis. Tensions began to increase, and over the next three days, violence began to spread as Whites marched into Colored Communities burning churches, schools, and homes. The violent clash between the two groups started three days of riots in Memphis, Tennessee. The three days of rioting was later known as the Memphis Massacre. As a result of the three days of violence, several areas in the Colored community were destroyed. Pa made sure we were safe. After two days of violence, General Stoneman ordered both Colored and White Soldiers on the afternoon of May 3, 1866 to re-establish order in the city and end the violence through martial law.

Many felt that the Memphis Massacre had a strong influence on the endorsement of the 14th Amendment to the Constitution, thus making all ex-slaves' citizens. He told Ma and me to start packing our things because he wanted us to move to Chicago with the hope for a better life. Daddy had a horse and wagon that we used to start our journey.

It took us a few days to pack up our lives. We spent long days on the road and cold nights sleeping in makeshift tents. I would stare up at the stars at night and imagine what life would be like in Chicago. Traveling to Chicago was not easy, but I was happy when we finally made it. Once we got there, life was better, but it was not as perfect as we had all imagined. It was still difficult for Pa to find a job. He searched for months to find a job. Many European Immigrants were competing with Colored People for labor jobs, and it was difficult for him. Colored Folks received opposition from the immigrants who felt we were a threat to them. Ma got a job cooking for a White Family. Pa eventually found work.

I was able to go to school. I was glad I was able to attend school after we moved from Memphis. The school was full of children of different sizes and ages, and we were all eager to learn. After school each day, I would teach Ma and Pa what I had learned. I started writing down the memories I had from my earlier years in Memphis. I wanted to keep a record of my life. I remembered Pa would tell people stories of the plantation that I wanted to remember when I got older and write about in my family history.

After years of living in Chicago, I was able to meet a nice man named Mike. Mike and I got married, we had a son named Mike Jr. and a daughter named Isabelle. Isabelle inherited the love I had for writing about important events in my life. Mike and I continued to be active in our local church and lived in a nice Colored community. Mike worked as a blacksmith, and I stayed at home with the kids. I enjoyed living in an incredibly supportive community and felt that things were going to gradually get better.

Even though we lived in Chicago, Colored People were still treated differently from the Whites. Several organizations such as the NAACP and Urban League, established chapters across the country that fought against injustices against Colored People. I remember the day that changed my life. I stopped at my neighbor Jamie's house for a quick visit. Jamie said,

"Sallie come in." I want you to meet someone, she just moved here from Memphis. I told her that your family moved here from Memphis years ago."

I walked in, and Jamie introduced me to Ida B. Wells. I was shocked. I had heard so many things about Mrs. Wells-Barnett.

Jamie asked me to sit down, and she brought us tea. We sat and talked for hours. She shared how she bought a first-class ticket, and the white train conductor asked her to move to the black section. Ida refused to move, and they tried to force her to move. She said,

"I bit him so hard." We all laughed.

Jaime said, "I guess he left you alone."

"I decided to sue the company" Ida replied, "I sued the train company for unfair treatment. I won, but later it was overturned."

I told her that I really admired her courage. I asked her what made her start writing about lynching across the South. She said,

"I had some friends who owned the People's Grocery Store, and when some Whites came and attacked them, they got mad and fought back. They later got arrested, and a White Mob got them out of jail and lynched them. After that, I wanted everyone to know about the injustice of lynching. So, I started traveling around the South investigating and telling stories about lynching. One day while I was away traveling, A White Mob incensed by my articles that were featured in Memphis Free Speech and Headlight office destroying all my equipment. I was warned not to return to Memphis. I was forced to move, I moved to New York, but I moved here in 1893." I told her, "we moved here after the Memphis Massacre."

"I am so honored to meet you, and if you need anything, I live next door to Jamie," I said. Ida laughed,

"Thanks, it is nice to meet you too."

Ida helped formed the National Association of Colored Women's Club chapter in Chicago, which I became an active member.

My daughter Isabelle had a history of her own, and it gave all our stories a deeper meaning.

Isabelle:

One Sunday in July 1919, my family decided to go to the 31st Street Beach families spend their Sunday afternoons after church. The colored people had an area, and the Whites had theirs. Suddenly, we heard a commotion from the other side of the beach. I did not realize that our friend Johnny from the neighborhood had drifted to the White side of the lake. Some White youth were yelling at him and started throwing stones at him. Johnny got hit in the head with a large stone and ended up drowning.

The Colored Folks' Community was outraged and demanded that the police act against the people who were throwing stones at Johnny. The police refused to take any action against the people that killed Johnny. Many colored people started meeting and said that it was time for "us" to take matters into "our" own hands. There were talks of protests and riots. I heard some people say that if the police will not do anything, they would. Then the riots started. The riots and violence went on for thirteen days. Mommy said that summer, many other cities had similar events. It was called the Red Summer of 1919 because of the bloodshed and death of over 1000 people.

Pa's boss found out that he was involved in the protest and other events that had occurred after Johnny's drowning and fired him. This was bad because our family depended on his income for survival. I overheard my parents in the kitchen talking about moving further North to find work. My parents decided to move to New York and stay with my Uncle Oscar until they could find a job and their own place to live. We all heard a lot of great things were happening in New York for Colored Folks, and my entire family was excited about the move. Besides, I was a little scared of what could happen to us after seeing Johnny and others killed.

After we arrived in New York, I stepped off the train and was amazed at the sharply dressed Colored People walking around the train station. They wore fancy suits and dresses with hats and shoes to match. I figured they all had to be rich because of their fancy clothes. Uncle Oscar met us at the train station. He was dressed like everyone else at the train station. After we got to his house, He told my Ma, about how things were so much different in New York than in the South.

"I tell you, Sallie, Colored Folks are doing big things in New York City. They have singers, poets, and other entertainers that you could pay to see. Colored people here have pride and openly express how they feel in their poems and music, and they are not scared. I tell you, Sallie it is beautiful. Well, I said all that to say: Welcome to New York. You have to get the kids in school, and we have to find you and Mike a job."

We moved to New York during the time that many newly freed slaves from the South, many Colored People from different Caribbean Islands, and European Immigrants were moving to New York in search of a better life. New York was a city of people from different cultures. The Colored People were encouraged to express themselves and to fight against the stereotypes that the world has placed on them.

My parents were getting used to their new life. It appeared that we had moved to New York during the perfect time between the 1920s to the mid-1930s, this time was later known as the Harlem Renaissance. The Harlem Renaissance gave birth to several famous entertainers such as Langston Hughes, Jacob Lawrence, Zora Neale Hurston, and Billie Holiday. My parents were able to get jobs at a Negro owned restaurant. I was impressed that so many Negro professionals attended my church and lived in my neighborhood. As I got older, I would often stop by the restaurant and get me something to eat. One day I met a man named Mark who worked at the restaurant with my parents. Mark was different he was knowledgeable about world events and I enjoyed talking to him. Mike and I start dating and got married a year after we met.

Mark met a man by the name of Charles Johnson while he was working at the restaurant. Pa met the man as well and said the man was impressed with his life story. He was passionate with his views on Negro Culture. Mark had a love for reading and writing and always talked about the injustices towards Negros. Mr. Johnson offered Mark a job, you would have thought Mark found a pot of gold. Mark started working at Opportunity Magazine.

Mark admired Mr. Johnson so much that we named our son Charles. While Mark worked at Opportunity Magazine, several great writers wrote for the magazine such as Langston Hughes and Zora Mae Hurston. I believe that because Charles watched so many influential people in the Negro Community, he was motivated to study and work hard to do well in school. Mark and I were determined our son would be someone great.

When Charles got accepted into college, Mike and I were the proudest parents in New York. Mike would tell everybody,

"Our boy is going to college."

What concerned us both was that he was going to school in the South. Charles was going to Fisk University. New York race relations were not perfect, but I was scared for my baby to go to school alone, especially in the South. I remember the day we sent Charles off to school. I packed a bible in Charles's bag. I tried to hold my tears back when he got on the train. I did not want him to see that I was scared for him. I wanted him to live out his dreams.

Charles said that he enjoyed meeting people from all parts of America. He loved the students and professors at Fisk, but he had to learn the unwritten rules of traveling in the South. Charles met a nice girl from Nashville, who was studying to be a teacher. He often wrote to me about some parts of Nashville that he was not allowed to be caught in. I was glad that Charles met someone who was from the area that helped him get adjusted to his new environment.

My husband and I were so proud that Charles was not only the first person in our family to attend and graduate from Fisk College and he was determined to fulfill his dream by becoming a doctor. Charles was accepted into Meharry Medical School in Nashville, Tennessee. My baby always said he wanted to become a doctor. After he graduated from Meharry, Charles took a job to work in Memphis at John Gaston Hospital. The whole family was ecstatic. The family felt good that he would be working in Memphis. Pa and Ma still knew some people who still lived in Memphis, they could not wait to tell people their grandson was a doctor. Charles married his college sweetheart, Mary. Mary and Charles had two children: Sandra and Lisa.

Lisa continued to write our history. I was glad the next generation would be documented,

Lisa:

My father came back from the NAACP Education meeting. He informed my mother that the NAACP had plans to desegregate Memphis City Schools with thirteen first graders. He asked my mother if she would let me become one of the students. When I heard him say that my heart dropped. I wanted to go to school with my friends in the neighborhood. I did not want to go to an all-White school. I was not sure how the teachers and students would treat me. I had heard stories about how Whites mistreated Blacks.

My father and mother discussed a list of parents who were considering sending their children to one of the four schools. He named my best friend, Diane. I thought maybe it would not be so bad if Diane would be with me. I overheard my mother say,

"Charles, no. Lisa is our baby. You know it will be too hard for her. She is only five years old. Things down here are different than New York. Charles, just imagine how things would be for her."

I did not hear anything for a minute or so, then my Daddy said,

"Yeah, Mary, you're right. I just wanted our child to have an opportunity for the best education. You know they do not give the students at black schools the best books."

My mom said, "I understand your concerns Charles, but just think about what is best for our child. At Brown Street School, the teachers love and genuinely care for those students. Mrs. Black would always let me know how Sandra was doing at school, and she still checks on her every now and then."

Diane and I were playing a week after my parent's conversation about the NAACP sending the thirteen students to Bridgetown an all-White school. Diane said,

"I am going to another school."

I asked her, "So we will not be at the same school?"

Diane said, "No, my Dad thinks I will make history by going to Bridgetown School. We will be the first ones to do it here in Memphis. He said I would help make things better for all Black Children in Memphis." I asked her how she felt about going, and Diane said, "Lisa, I am scared, really scared." I hugged her and told her it would be okay.

Memphis leaders did not want to draw attention to the integration of Memphis City Schools. The Board of Education and the NAACP did not identify the name of the schools. Days before the students transferred to their new school. Diane's parents received many threats from angry Whites who were against Blacks and Whites going to school together. Diane's and my preparation for school was slightly different. Daddy took me to school, and Diane's father and the police had to escort her to school. Mrs.

James greeted us at the door like she does every morning. Today, I could not stay focused. I could not stop thinking about Diane and how her first day at her new school was going. I hope she liked her new teacher and that she made some new friends. The transition was successful compared to other cities President John Kennedy acknowledged their calm integration.

Later that day, Daddy picked me up from school. I told him I enjoyed my day. When we pulled up in the driveway, I saw Diane and her father just sitting in the car. Diane slowly got out of the car with tears in her eyes. I called her name and waved at her. She just put up her hand, then she stopped and started to run towards me. She hugged me tight while she was crying. Her father called her to go into the house.

My Daddy said, "Sam let the girls spend a little time with each other. I will stay out here to watch them. Sam, are you okay?"

Mr. James just shook his head to say yes and walked into the house. Diane and I walked towards my house and sat on the porch. Diane said,

"Lisa, I do not want to go back to that school."

"Diane, what happened?" I asked.

John was so scared he wet his pants. The police had to walk us into the school and walk me to class. My teacher was mean to me. During recess, one of the students kept standing behind me and calling me the bad N-word while throwing rocks at me. My teacher, Mrs. Jefferson, only told him to stop throwing rocks. I could not wait for the school day to end." She started crying and said, "I do not want to go back to that school..."

It was starting to get late, so my Dad and I walked her back to her house. Later that night, I told my parents about Diane's first day at her new school. Mommy said,

"Charles, I told you that I did not want Lisa to go through that."

"I asked James if Diane will continue to go to that school. He stressed that he wanted society to know that his child had as much right to attend that school as any child," my Dad replied. The next day, I watched my friend as she left to go to school. I could see the tears in her eyes. I wish I understood how much this was helping other Black Children to have a better future. I hated to see her sad, I was proud of Diane and the other kids for standing up to those mean people every day.

I remember hearing how others took a stand and demanded equal rights. I heard people talking about the Children's Crusade in Birmingham, AL. On May 2, 1963, students staged a walkout of their classrooms and marched throughout the streets of Birmingham. There were over a thousand Black Children who participated in the walkout. Many of these children were put in jail and were attacked by dogs and water hoses. Even though the children faced horrible treatments, they continued to protest. I admired the fact that they wanted a better life for themselves and other Black Children. I wanted to do something myself to help make life better for other Blacks.

Years have passed since my last journal entry, but the city's race relations remained the same. There are still Black only and

White only signs to separate the races. Leaders like Martin Luther King Jr., Rosa Parks, and Malcolm X were vocal about demanding that all races should have equal rights and equal treatment. My parents would often listen to Martin Luther King Jr's speeches on the radio. One-night, Daddy returned from a NAACP meeting and told us that the Southern Christian Leadership Conference (SCLC) was having Martin Luther King Jr. to return to Memphis to continue the march to protest the treatment of the Memphis Sanitation Workers. After he told us I screamed,

"Daddy, I want to march too! I want to meet Dr. King!"

Daddy said, "Baby girl, you know it will be a lot of people out there. I do not think you will be able to get close enough to meet him. I do not think it is a good idea for you to go, but I did hear them mention that he will be speaking at Mason Temple on Wednesday night. We all can go to hear him speak as a family." Hearing that made me so excited I could hardly sleep just thinking about hearing him in person.

The day finally came, and I wanted to wear my best dress. That Wednesday night there was an intense thunderstorm. The crow braved the stormy weather all were anxious to hear Dr. King speak. My mother, father, my sister Sandra dressed and headed to Mason Temple. After we got there, I was glad we were able to get a good seat. My eyes were focused on Dr. King during his entire speech. While he was speaking, I had a feeling that things would get better not only in Memphis but all over this country. After his speech, Sandra told my parents how much she appreciated the opportunity to hear Dr. King speak. I agreed.

It was on a Thursday morning. April 4, 1968. My mother got me ready for school, as usual. My father was planning to march with Dr. King later that day to protest the treatment of the sanitation workers. I wanted to participate in the march too, but since my Daddy allowed me to hear him speak the previous night, I felt like that was good enough. I knew my Daddy did not know that Sandra planned to march too. She got dressed as though she was going to class, but she was planning to meet with her friends at school to march. I hoped Daddy would not see her there. If he did, she would be in big trouble. Our parents were for the march and its purpose, but they were afraid of some of the things that could happen to people during the march. They loved and did not want to see us get hurt.

My day at school was different. I could not stop thinking about what was going on at the march. Grandma picked me up after school and we went to her house. We watched the news while they showed clips of the march. Suddenly, breaking news came across the screen, announcing that Dr. King had been shot. My grandmother could not stop crying. I felt sad. I could not understand why someone would want to shoot him. He always preached about nonviolence, but he was a victim of violence. That was something I could not understand. I asked my grandmother why someone would want to hurt Dr. King. She looked at me with tears in her eyes and said,

"Baby, some people do not want people of different races to live and work together equally. Some people just have hate in their hearts, but not everybody is like that. Some White People are active in the fight for equal rights for Blacks too. I just hope that we continue to fight for justice and equal rights. We all have a little Dr. King in us, even you." She hugged and kissed me on the forehead. After she said that, I thought about what I could do to help fight for equal rights for all. Just because I am eleven years old, I can help make a difference. The children in Birmingham marched in Children Crusade. I am sure there is something I can do here in Memphis.

My mother and father arrived at my grandmother's house to pick me up. They both confirmed that Dr. King had died. My father had this blank look on his face like he saw a ghost. My mother kept saying,

"He is gone; he is gone."

I did not want to say anything. I just got my books, kissed my grandmother, and walked out of the house. When we got home, Sandra was still not there. My parents began to worry about her safety, but she walked in thirty minutes later. She never mentioned where she had been, and they did not ask. They were happy that she was home safe. The news of Dr. King's death angered the Black Community. Riots broke out in Memphis and many other cities. My parents did not want me to go to school the next few days in fear that something may happen. On April 8, 1968, Mrs. Coretta Scott King, Dr. King's wife, arranged another march to the mayor's office to address the demands of the sanitation union. I remember seeing her marching with a black lace headscarf with her children by her side. The next day, they had Dr. King's funeral in Atlanta, Georgia.

As years passed, I was determined to remain active in my community. I attended Clark College and became an active member in the local NAACP, student government, and Pre-Law Society. My childhood experiences encouraged me to major in

26

Political Science After I graduated from Clark College, I attended the Thurgood Marshall Law School in Houston, Texas. I graduated three years later and met my husband, Lee. Lee and I discovered that we both had a strong passion to help our community. Lee and I would volunteer on weekends feeding the homeless and helped and support each other with school. Lee was originally from Chicago and had family members who lived in Memphis. After we got married, we were both fortunate to land jobs in Memphis, so we decided to move to Memphis. We had two beautiful children, Jamal, and Jessica.

Jessica continued the family history of storytelling through her journal.

Jessica:

I decided to follow mother's footsteps and attend her alma mater Clark College that is now Clark Atlanta University. She would always talk about her experience at Clark College and being a part of the Atlanta University Center (AUC), which included Morehouse College, Morris Brown College, Spelman College, Morehouse School of Medicine, and the Interdenominational Theological Center (ITC).

It was August of 1991 when I was a freshman at Clark Atlanta University. I was amazed to meet people from all over the world: all 50 states, Africa, The Islands, and other countries. They all looked like me but had different life experiences. During my freshman week, we had several activities where we interacted with not only with Clark Atlanta students but students from the other schools in the AUC as well. My parents were shocked to see how quickly I adjusted to college. They were surprised that I was not calling them as much as they felt I would.

On the last day of our freshman week, students from all the schools met for an assembly to listen to several motivational speakers. They stated several times how important it was to make our next four-years count. They told us that we have an obligation to pull someone up with us after we graduate. They reminded us that we were standing on the shoulders of our ancestors and had an obligation to be successful. As I returned to my dorm room that night, I had no doubt that I made the right choice by attending Clark Atlanta University.

My best friend, James was a freshman at Morehouse. Our mothers both had attended Clark College, and they were best friends. Our parents made us promise them that we would take care of each other while we were in Atlanta. On April 29,1992 James and I were watching TV in his dorm room breaking news came on, The Rodney King verdict was announced, three of the police officers were acquitted in the beating of Rodney King, Mark, who was from Compton, busted into the room and asked,

"Did you see what happened in LA?" We answered that we did.

Mark said, "They cannot do this to us. My homeboys said people are going crazy in LA." Mark kept pacing the floor and saying, "We have to make a point." James and I just looked at him.

James said, "No, we do not. Besides, what are you talking about?"

Mark said, "I can't just sit here" and asked James if he was coming with him.

James told Mark, "I need to walk Jessica back to her dorm."

Mark left the room in a rage. While we were walking back to my dorm, I guess the news had spread. It was a very weird feeling that night. While we were walking back to my dorm, James started sounding like he agreed with Mark.

I asked James, "You are not thinking about joining Mark tonight, are you?" I reminded him that we had promised our parents that we would take care of each other and stay out of trouble.

James looked down and said, "You are right. I need to get started on my paper anyway." James and I hugged, and he walked back to his dorm.

Later that night a couple of students from the AUC marched to the City Hall. Over the next couple of days many several local stores, including the university's bookstore, were vandalized. After things settled down, things eventually got back to normal. The bookstore covered their windows, but it was still in operation. Some stores remained closed for a few days, and many never opened again in that area.

My parents came to Atlanta to visit me. They noticed that the bookstore was boarded up. My father stared at the students who were in line to sell their books back.

He said to me. "You all looted the bookstore, and now you are all trying to sell your books back. That does not make sense." He looked at me and shook his head. I took my parents around and introduced them to my friends. My mother wanted to walk around the campus to see how much things had changed since she graduated. Afterwards, we went to my favorite soul food restaurant that was near campus. My mother used to eat there when she was in school. I was excited not to have to eat in the cafeteria for dinner.

While at Clark Atlanta University, I started out as a Biology Major, but since Chemistry and I did not want to be my friends, I decided to change my major to history. I really enjoyed my history classes, especially Mr. Jones's classes. Mr. Jones was a doctoral candidate at Clark Atlanta University from Liberia. I enjoyed listening to his stories about his country and why he had an American last name. He was a descendent of free slaves from America who relocated to Liberia. Several years before Slavery ended, there was a Colony Society that included James Monroe and Andrew Jackson. They discussed what should happen if slaves gained freedom. For several years, the Colony Society secured and bought land in West Africa on what we know today as Liberia. My professor informed us that back then, his country was in turmoil because the descendants of the indigenous people were tired of descendants from America or the Caribbean ruling their country. In 1980 Master Sargent Samuel Doe staged the assignation of President William Tolbert. After this, there was a lot of tension in his country of Liberia. I always enjoyed the personal knowledge my professor shared with the class. I genuinely enjoyed my experience at Clark Atlanta University. I would not have traded it for anything in the world. My dad had told me that the friends I met in college would prove to be my dearest friends. This appears to be true.

It has been a while since I wrote in my journal, but my college adventures could fill several journals. After I graduated in 1995, I moved back home to Memphis, where I met my husband, Malik. I met Malik when I was walking down the aisle of a grocery store. I had on my Clark Atlanta University T-shirt, and he stopped me and asked if I knew his cousin Kelly Bryant. I said, "Yeah, we stayed in the same freshman dorm." We started to realize that we knew some of the same people. Malik graduated from Howard

31

University and was enrolled at the University of Tennessee Medical School when we met. We got married in 1997 and had a son named Amari and a daughter Imani.

My son Amari kept a journal of his own, and the story of our family continued.

Amari:

Ms. Jackson asked our class to start writing about our most memorable experiences and add to it as we grow. I started writing when I was in fifth grade. My parents and I were watching the news, and the breaking news alert came across the screen. The United States Senator Barack Obama from Illinois had just announced his candidacy for President for the 2008 election. Mommy said,

"You see that Amari, I told you can be whatever you want to be, even the President of the United States." She then added, "Look at that, an African- American Man running for President of the United States."

Daddy said, "You know he is not the first African-American to run for President, right?" Mommy had a strange look on her face.

She said, "Yeah, I know,"

Daddy responded, "Ok, name them."

"Name them?" Mommy asked. "Okay," she said, "Jesse Jackson!"

Daddy said, "Ok, he is one."

"There are more?" I asked.

"Yes," Daddy said, "There was George Edwin in 1904, Shirley Chisholm in 1972, Lenora Fulani in 1988, and I bet you did not know Frederick Douglas".

Mommy and I both said at the same time, "Frederick Douglas?"

"Yes, Frederick Douglas spoke at the Republican Convention in 1888, and he received a nomination for presidency from the floor after a called vote".

I said, "Dad, I thought Frederick Douglas was a slave."

Daddy said, "Well, son, he was born into Slavery and later he became an abolitionist. An abolitionist was a person who spoke out against Slavery."

Mommy said, "Well, I guess you just told us something."

We all laughed. A few minutes later, Grandma called, and I answered the phone. I could hear the excitement in her voice,

"Did you hear that a Black man is running for President?"

I said, "Yes, Grandma, I did. We just saw it on the news."

She said, "Baby let me speak to your mother." I gave the phone to my mother, and she informed my mother that she planned to start working on registering people to vote. Grandma told Mommy, which were some folks her age and older who did not vote.

She told my Mommy, "That is a shame because they are old enough to know what we Black Folks had to get the right the right to vote."

As months past, Grandma kept her word and spent many days volunteering at our local Obama campaign headquarters. She even convinced our pastor to have a voter registration table after church. If Grandma found out that someone was not registered to vote, she would tell them, "Now baby, you know that your ancestors were beaten, hosed, and attacked for trying to protest for their rights to vote. Now we do not have to go through all that, so we owe it to them to get out and vote."

I do not think you all understand how important it is to vote. Did you all know in 1866, the Civil Rights Bill was created to give Black Americans rights as a citizen which included having the right to vote? President Andrew Johnson vetoed the bill, but Congress overrode it, and it passed. Over a span of ten years, there were as many as sixteen Black elected Congressmen and two Senators. The sad thing is that many states started to create qualifications such as literacy tests, poll taxes, threats, and other discriminating tactics to prevent Blacks from voting. It was not until Lynden Johnson signed the Voting Rights Act in 1966 that banned having literacy tests and other discriminatory practices to prevent Blacks from voting. That is why we need to vote. If they were able to elect sixteen Black Congressmen, shortly after

Slavery imagine what we can do now. Your vote is important because the people we place in office make decisions that affect your life. Okay, I will stop preaching I am just passionate about exercising your right to vote."

Voters had an opportunity to vote in the Democratic primary race. During the time of the primary races, our television stayed on the news channel. On June 7, 2008, an announcement was made that Barack Obama was nominated as the Democratic candidate for President. Mommy looked at the television with a smile on her face and said,

"Well, he is a step closer to becoming President."

Grandma was at our house watching the news channel with us. She said,

"You all," jokingly, "I am getting ready to really get busy now." Grandma continued her work with the local Obama Campaign drive and working with voter registration.

November 4, 2008 was a much-anticipated day for many not only African Americans but, people who wanted a political change. That day Mommy woke me up early and said,

"Amari, I want you to go with me to vote. Then I will take you to school"

Even though we got there by 6:50 a.m., they were a lot of people standing in line and waiting for the doors to open for them to vote. After waiting for thirty minutes, Mommy came out with her, *I voted* sticker on her jacket. She said,

"Well, Amari, we will see what will happen later on tonight."

We arrived at my school, and she asked me, "Amari, do you think Barak Obama will be our next president?" I shrugged my shoulders. I honestly did not know what the outcome of that day's election would be, but I wanted him to win. That night our television stayed on the news channel. I tried to stay up and watch the results but ended up falling asleep. I woke up to loud cheers. I woke up and asked,

"What happened"?

Mommy said, "Baby, he won! Barack Obama will be our next President." Grandma called; I could hear her through the phone.

"He won! He won! -We are ready to have our first Black President!"

Grandma was determined to attend the Inauguration in Washington, D.C. The next day Grandma called Pastor Jones to ask if the church would be interested in chartering a bus to attend the Inauguration. Pastor Jones agreed, and the next few months, Grandma started getting the information together to prepare for the trip. Months later, 120 people from Green Stone Baptist Church traveled from Memphis, Tennessee to Washington, D.C., to witness the first Black President being sworn in as President of the United States of American. We got to Washington, and it was a beautiful sight. I had never been to Washington, D.C. before. I saw several monuments that I read about in school. So many people traveled from all over the world to witness this event.

When we got to the Capitol Building and the National Mall, people were everywhere. We were not able to get close, but they had screens near the stage so everyone would be able to see. I was so excited and inspired to see so many famous people in attendance and speaking at the Inauguration. Then the moment that everyone had been waiting on: witnessing Barack Obama being sworn in as the 44th President of United States of America. While he was being sworn in, I looked at my Grandma. I noticed that she had tears in her eyes. I asked her, "Why are you crying?" She said, "Amari, I thought I would never see the day when we would have a Black President in this country. We have been through so much as a people, and to see this, it is amazing. Baby, these are tears of joy."

When I returned to school, I was glad my teacher asked me to write about my experience attending the Inauguration.

It has been some years since my last letter. I cannot believe that my Grandma is no longer here. I am glad we were able to spend time with her and share that memory of seeing the first Black President winning not once but twice. I guess I can add my letters to the box, and hopefully, future generations will continue the Johnson legacy and become a part of history.

Appendix

Juan Garrido traveled with Juan Ponce de Leon in 1513 on his expedition to Florida in search of the Fountain of Youth.

In 1526 enslaved Africans arrived at Roanoke Island on the Sir Francis Drake's Fleet. The Africans later revolted.

August 1619, enslaved Africans arrived in Virginia.

June 19, 1865, when Major General Gordon Granger arrived in Galveston, Texas to announce the end of the war and the end of slavery which is known as Juneteenth.

October 3, 1961, the thirteen first graders who intergraded Memphis City Schools. The four schools were Bruce Elementary, Gorgon Elementary, Rozelle Elementary, and Springdale Elementary.

Bruce Elementary students: Dwania Kyles, Harry Williams, Michael Willis

Gordon Elementary students: Alvin Freeman, Sharon Malone, Shelia Malone, and Pamela Mays

Rozelle Elementary students: Jayce Bell, F. C. Freeman, Leandrew Wiggins and Clarence Williams

Springdale Elementary students: Deborah Ann Holt and Jacqueline Moore

Black Members of The House of Representatives during Reconstruction 1863 -1877

Alabama
Jeremiah Haralson
James T. Rapier
Benjamin S. Turner

Florida
Isaiah T. Walls

Georgia
Jefferson Long

Louisiana
Charles Nash

Mississippi
Hiram Rhodes Revels – Senator
Blanche Kelso Bruce- Senator

North Carolina
John A. Hyman

South Carolina
Richard H. Cain
Robert C. De Large
Robert B. Elliot
Joseph H. Rainey
Alonzo J. Ransier
Robert Smalls

References.

Branston, John (2004, May 19). Integration and Innocence. Memphis Flyer. Retrieved from http//www.memphisflyer.com/Memphis/integration-and innocence/content.

Gates, Henry Lewis (2012, October 22), Who was the First African American, The Root, retrieved from www.theroot.com/whowasthefirstafricanamerica-79089308.

Gilmore, Kim (2020, January 28). The Birmingham Children's Crusade of 1963. Biography. Retrieved from www.biography.com/news/black-history-birmingham-childrens-crusade-1963.

Higgins, Abigail (2019, June 26). Red Summer of 1919: How Black WW1 Vets Fought Back Against Racist Mobs. History.

Kiel, Daniel (2014, June 23). The First Graders who were "The Memphis 13" A Different visual Take on Brown v. Board, Doc and Law.

Kiel, Daniel (2008). Exploded Dream: Desegregation in the Memphis City Schools. A journal of Theory and Practice volume 26 issue 2 Article 1.

Little, Becky (2019, April 5) How a Movement to Send Freed Slaves to Africa created Liberia. Retrieved from http//www.history.comnews/slavery-american-colonization-society Liberia,

Norwood, Arlisha (2017). Ida B. Wells-Barnett (1862-1931). Retrieved from http//www.womenshistory, org/education-resources/biographies/Ida b wells Barnett.

Patterson, Tiffany (2020, January 3). What Everyone Should Know about Reconstruction 150 years after the 15th Amendment's ratification, West Virginia University Associated Press.

Ponti, Crystal (2019, August 26). America's History of Slavery Began Long Before Jamestown-The Arrival of the First Captives to the Jamestown Colony, in 1619 is often seen as the Beginning of Slavery in America-but Enslaved African Arrived in North America as Early as the 1500s. History, retrieved from www.history.com/news/american-slavery-before-Jamestown-1619.

Rosenbloom, Joseph. (2018, April 4), Martin Luther King's Last 31 hours: The Story of his Final Prophetic Speech. The Guardian.

Schermerhorn Calvin. (2018, May 8). Civil Rights Do Not Always Stop Racism Although the 1866 Memphis Massacre

Happed 150 years ago, it Still has a Powerful Legacy in the South. Retrieved from www.theatlantic.com.

Andrew Johnson and the Emancipation in Tennessee (2020, February 5). National Historical Site. Retrieved from www.nps.gov/anjo/learn/historyculture/johnson-and-tn-emanicipation.htm.

www.ingramcontent.com/pod-product-compliance
Lightning Source LLC
Chambersburg PA
CBHW031904170626
46807CB00004B/1891

* 9 7 8 1 7 3 5 2 5 9 3 0 7 *